CHILLERS

The Real Porky Philips

Mark Haddon

PUFFIN BOOKS

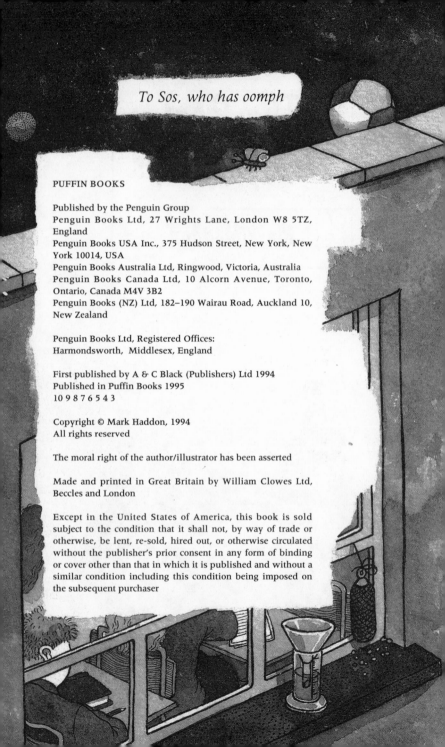

To Sos, who has oomph

PUFFIN BOOKS

Published by the Penguin Group
Penguin Books Ltd, 27 Wrights Lane, London W8 5TZ,
England
Penguin Books USA Inc., 375 Hudson Street, New York, New
York 10014, USA
Penguin Books Australia Ltd, Ringwood, Victoria, Australia
Penguin Books Canada Ltd, 10 Alcorn Avenue, Toronto,
Ontario, Canada M4V 3B2
Penguin Books (NZ) Ltd, 182–190 Wairau Road, Auckland 10,
New Zealand

Penguin Books Ltd, Registered Offices:
Harmondsworth, Middlesex, England

First published by A & C Black (Publishers) Ltd 1994
Published in Puffin Books 1995
10 9 8 7 6 5 4 3

Made and printed in Great Britain by William Clowes Ltd,
Beccles and London

Chapter One

Wobbly Bits

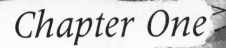

So, who would like to play the genie?

asked Miss Cardigan, putting on her glasses and looking round the class. "Any offers?"

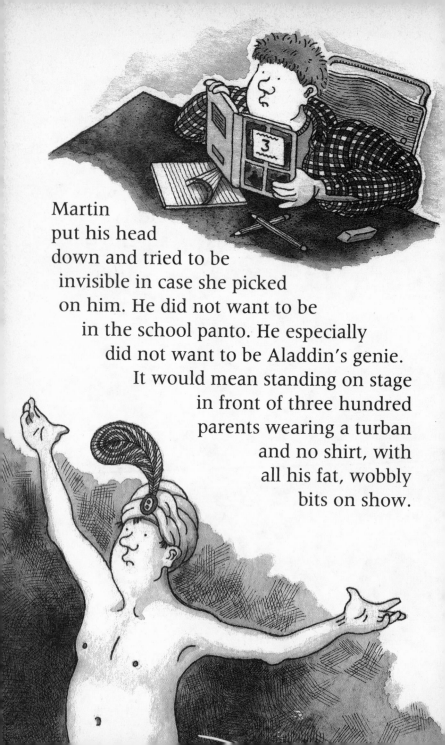

Martin
put his head
down and tried to be
invisible in case she picked
on him. He did not want to be
in the school panto. He especially
did not want to be Aladdin's genie.
It would mean standing on stage
in front of three hundred
parents wearing a turban
and no shirt, with
all his fat, wobbly
bits on show.

Martin Philips!

said Miss Cardigan cheerily, walking
towards him like a hungry tiger,
"What about you?"

"Well . . . I . . . I mean . . ." he
stammered, blushing.

"Come on," she laughed, "it'll be fun."

5

Martin looked round, hoping someone
else might want to play the genie.
No luck. Everyone was smirking.
They could see he didn't want to play
the part. They were imagining him on
stage with all his wobbly bits on show.

They thought it was a really good joke.

shouted Sarah Butts.

Miss Cardigan told her to stop being rude, but her voice was drowned out by the rest of the class chanting, "Do it! Do it! Do it!"

"Well, Martin, it looks like you've got fans already," she smiled. "What do you say?"

Martin wanted to say, "They're *not* fans." But the only words which squeaked out of his mouth were

Alright, then.

The class cheered.

"Porky . . ." Martin said to himself, "that was *really* stupid."

At lunch, Tudge came up behind Martin and said,

So, you're in the show, too?

slapping him on the back and making Martin choke on a spoonful of bread pudding. "Welcome aboard, Porky. It's going to be a hoot."

It was alright for kids like Tudge. Nothing scared him. He had a black belt in judo. He had been caught shoplifting.

He had been suspended for taking a wheel off the headmaster's Vauxhall Cavalier. After that, playing Aladdin was a doddle.

"Hey," grinned Kevvy, Tudge's mate, "it's not the end of the world."

"Feels like it," grumbled Martin.

He wasn't a big-mouth, tearaway show-off. He didn't like being the centre of attention. He liked things quiet and simple. In fact, right now, he wanted to fade away into thin air so that he would never have to think about the panto again.

9

At supper that night, Trish swept her long, black hair out of her eyes and announced,

I'm playing the Sultan's daughter.

"The Sultan's daughter is absolutely, incredibly, amazingly beautiful. I was the obvious choice."

"If your head gets any bigger you won't get through the front door," said Mum. "Now finish your tea and wipe the tomato sauce off your chin."

"Are you OK, buster?" asked Dad, turning to Martin who was sitting prodding his scampi round his plate.

"Yeh," he replied, not meaning it.

Mum slotted her plate into the dishwasher and patted his shoulder. "What's up, love?"

"I've got to play the genie," admitted Martin in a tiny voice.

"But why didn't you tell me before?" smiled Mum. "That's grand. Two little stars in the family. My, my!"

Trish's jaw fell open.
"*What?!*" she screeched.
"You? The genie?
That's a joke!"

"Walk under a lorry,"
said Martin quietly.

"Less of that, you
cheeky madam,"
barked Dad,
shaking a slice
of bread at her.

Trish stood up in a monstrous huff and
said, "You'll wreck that panto. I am *not*
sharing the same stage as my little toe-rag
of a brother." And with that she
stormed out of the room like
a very spoilt Sultan's daughter.

"Take no notice
of Lady Muck,"
said Mum.
"You'll be a
knock-out."

That evening, Martin stood in the
bathroom booming at the mirror.

Greetings,
Master!

I am the
genie of the
oil~lamp.
Your every
wish is my
command.

He was wearing
his racing-car patterned boxer-
shorts and a tea-towel wrapped
round his head; and he had
turned the taps on so no-one would
hear him. The lines were easy,
and he sounded good locked inside
the bathroom. But whenever he
thought about those bright lights, the
big hall and that massive audience
his legs went gooey, his mind
went blank and he wanted to be sick.

It had been a week now. He couldn't stop thinking about the panto. It was haunting him. It was following him round like a big, black shadow, weighing him down, not letting him sleep, giving him nightmares.

He told Miss Cardigan that he couldn't do it. He told her someone else could have the part. But she was having none of it.

"Don't worry. It's only nerves," she said soothingly.

"Can you die of nerves?" asked Martin.

But Miss Cardigan didn't think that was very funny.

Chapter Two

Weird Things

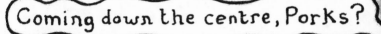

Coming down the centre, Porks?

asked Tudge, leaning over the fence.

"Nah . . ." said Martin. "Not right now."

Going down to the Centre with Tudge was asking for trouble. Chances were, he'd end up in a fight with kids from St Benedict's, or try putting a burger down someone's trousers, or persuade everyone to climb on to the roof of the bus station.

Besides, Martin had too much on his mind. He couldn't think about anything except the panto. No. He would stay at home and lie in bed and concentrate on getting measles or the flu or something.

"Suit yourself," muttered Kevvy. "Come on, Tudge." And they wandered off.

"What a weed!" said a voice.

Martin turned round. The voice belonged to Trish. "Some genie you'll make," she sneered. "Genies have guts. Genies have get-up-and-go. Genies have oomph. The fluff in my belly-button's got more oomph than you."

It was on Tuesday morning that the weird things started to happen.

Tudge passed him in the corridor and said, "Glad you came down the Centre, then?"

"What?" said Martin, because he hadn't gone down to the Centre.

"You were a scream, Porks," sniggered Tudge. "When you put that burger down the trousers of the snotty kid from St. Benedict's . . ." He was crying with laughter now, "I nearly wet myself. I've never seen anything so funny." He staggered away, wiping the tears from his eyes.

Martin didn't like it. Not one bit. Maybe Tudge was just joking. More likely, it was some sort of trick. He probably had some evil plan up his sleeve. Martin was worried.

It got worse. On Wednesday, Sarah Butts asked if he'd enjoyed the film the night before. But he hadn't been to the cinema.

On Thursday, Kevvy said it was a brilliant goal he'd scored when they were playing football up at the park the previous evening. But Martin hadn't been up at the park.

On Friday, Tudge said, "You've joined the swimming club at the sports complex, then?"

"Just stop it," said Martin, who was getting tired of this game.

Tudge gave him a weird look and said,

Why keep it a secret? I saw you on my way back from judo. I'd recognise you anywhere, Porks.

Martin badly wanted to know what everyone was up to.

He didn't like being kept in the dark. So, the next day, he finished breakfast quickly and headed down to the shopping mall, where Tudge and Kevvy always hung around on Saturday mornings. He'd get to the bottom of this once and for all.

He was just passing Tesco's when he saw them sitting round the fountain.

He stopped in his tracks. There was a new kid with them, a short, fat kid in a baseball jacket. There was something about the new kid that made Martin uncomfortable. His face looked familiar somehow. He didn't like the look of him.

Martin moved behind a pillar and watched.

After a few minutes, the new kid punched Tudge chummily on the shoulder and began walking away, towards Martin.

What was it? What was so creepy about him?

The new kid walked right past the pillar so that Martin was able to glance directly into his face. Suddenly, Martin knew why he looked familiar. Every inch of his skin froze. The new kid looked like him, *exactly* like him. He turned and began running after the new kid. He had to find out who he was.

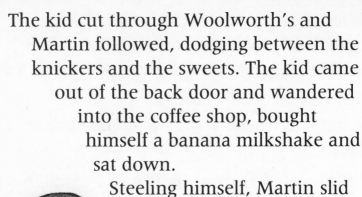

The kid cut through Woolworth's and
Martin followed, dodging between the
knickers and the sweets. The kid came
out of the back door and wandered
into the coffee shop, bought
himself a banana milkshake and
sat down.

Steeling himself, Martin slid
into the seat opposite him.

"Hi!" said the new kid.
"I've been expecting you."

"Who are you?"
stuttered Martin.
It was like
looking in a mirror.

It was like listening to your own echo.
And it was making his hair stand on end

"Martin Philips," said the new kid,
"otherwise known as Porky."

"But. . . !" Martin felt too weak
to say anything for a few seconds.
"But . . . you *can't* be."

"I'm afraid I can," said the
kid, rolling up his sleeve and
showing Martin his birth-
mark: a little, brown
Australia-shape on his
elbow, exactly the
same as Martin's.
"See?"

"But, *I'm* Martin Philips," insisted Martin, hoping that this was all just a bad dream and that he'd wake up soon.

"So am I," said the kid. "Except . . ."

Martin tried to reply but his throat had gone dry.

"Except," the kid continued, "I'm better at it."

Martin's voice came back suddenly. "At what?" he shouted, so loud that everyone in the coffee shop turned round to look.

"At being Porky Philips. I mean . . ." said the kid, leaning towards him across the table, "you let your sister bully you. You won't go down the Centre and have fun with Tudge and Kevvy. And you're going to be one major flop as Aladdin's genie."

Martin was speechless. It sounded horribly, horribly, true.

The kid finished his banana milkshake and got up to leave.

"What about *me*?" asked Martin, feeling small and useless.

"Oh, you . . ." said the kid, walking towards the door, "you'll just sort of fade away. Into thin air. It'll be great. No worries. No panto. Nothing. I'll handle all that."

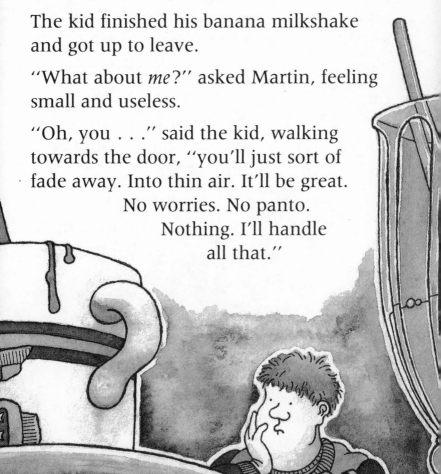

Chapter Three

Fading Away

He wanted to tell Mum. She knew something was bothering him. "What's the matter, pet?" she kept saying. "You're so quiet recently. Is anything wrong? Go on, tell me what's worrying you."

But he couldn't say anything. If he told the truth, she'd think he had gone bonkers. There was nothing he could say. So he kept his mouth shut.

It really did feel as if he was starting to disappear.

He couldn't concentrate at the rehearsal. He kept thinking about the meeting in the coffee-shop. He kept saying to himself, "You just imagined it. It's not real. It's impossible."

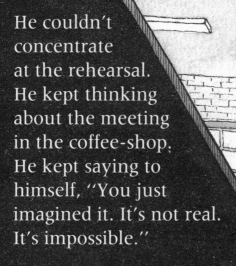

And then it was his cue.

"Look, Mother," said

Tudge rubbing the brass lamp, "there is a genie in here who will solve all our problems."

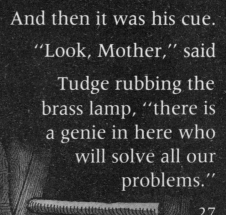

There wasn't going to be any real smoke until the night of the performance, so Martin just climbed up out of the hole in the stage, lifted up his arms and said, "Greetings Master. I am the genie of the oil-lamp. My every wish is your command."

Speak up, Martin!

shouted Miss Cardigan. "I can't hear a word you're saying!"

It's happening, thought Martin. I'm fading away already.

That evening, as he was lying in the bath, Trish barged in, washed her face, brushed her teeth, combed her hair then went out again while he lay there covering himself with his yellow flannel.

It was as if he didn't exist.

29

A few days before the panto, he was sitting at the back of the bus after school. Tudge and the gang were upstairs terrorising old ladies. He had almost forgotten the panto. It didn't matter now. Only one thing mattered. The other Porky Philips.

He hadn't imagined it. It was real. If it hadn't been for the birthmark, then maybe, just maybe, the kid could have been a long-lost brother, or twin or something. But the birthmark was *his* birthmark. The kid was him alright. The thought made Martin feel sick and dizzy, like you felt when you leant too far out of a very high window.

Which was how Martin was feeling when he saw the kid. He looked down the aisle of the bus and there he was. His hair. His ears. His baseball jacket. The double.

Martin knew he had to do something. But what? Hand him in to the police? Feed him a poisoned chocolate bar? Put him on a one-way plane to America?

The bus stopped
and the kid stood
up. Martin got
off and followed
him. He'd find
out where the
kid lived. That's
what he'd do.
Then, when he'd
done that . . .
Well, he'd think
of something.

The kid went into the park, walked round the swings and headed for the alleyway down the side of the garage. Martin hung back, keeping in the shadow of the trees.

When Martin reached the end of the alleyway he saw the back of the kid's baseball jacket disappear behind a post-box and head down Grenville Close. He ran to the post-box and watched for the kid's next move.

Martin was so busy following the kid that he didn't notice when they turned into his own road. Only when the kid opened the gate into Martin's garden did he suddenly realize what was happening. He started to run, but he was a hundred yards back. He tried to shout, but he was breathless from running. Up ahead of him, the kid rang the bell. Dad opened the door and let the kid in.

33

Martin sprinted to the end of the road, jumped over the wall and ran up to the front door. He reached out his hand to ring the bell, then stopped. What would happen when Dad came to the door? What would he say? What would *Dad* say? His hand flopped to his side.

He sneaked round the side of the house to the garden and glanced between the curtains of the lounge. Trish was hogging the sofa, filing her nails and the kid, the other Porky Philips, was eating his way through a packet of chocolate digestives.

Martin felt completely beaten.

He turned away from the window and wandered down to the bench at the bottom of the garden. He sat and looked back at the warm lights coming from the house. He turned his collar up. It was cold and he was getting hungry.

Slowly, night came down.

Chapter Four

Wormy Apples and Stale Bread

There was nothing he could do.

He wanted to go and ring the bell. But then what? How could Mum and Dad tell that he was the real Martin? The other kid had already fooled them. They would probably think *he* was the fake. They would shut the door on him, or send for the police, or have him taken away.

He was shivering. He needed to get warm before he froze to death. He crept round the back of Dad's shed, levered open the little window and clambered inside.

On the shelf were the apples and pears they'd picked from the two trees last month. He cut out the wormy bits with his biro and ate four of them. Then he wrapped himself in some old sacks and lay down to sleep on the fertilizer bags.

He woke up crumpled and dirty. His neck hurt from sleeping all curled up, and he was still shivering. He ate another apple and slipped up the garden to the back of the house.

Hiding behind the drainpipe, he sneaked a look into the kitchen. They were all in there. Dad was crunching toast behind the paper, Mum was scrambling eggs and the kid was eating out of Martin's very own stripey cereal bowl.

But that wasn't the worst of it. The kid turned to Trish and said something. Martin couldn't hear what it was, but it made her laugh. She threw her head back and showed all her big, white teeth.

Martin had never made Trish laugh in his entire life.

Mum smiled, ruffled the kid's hair and said something like, "You've certainly cheered up!"

Martin felt so angry he wanted to smash the window. It was bad enough that this kid, this creature, this thing, was taking over his life. But, to make matters worse, everyone liked him. Even Trish.

Who would want the real Porky Philips back now?

Porky squeezed
through
the hedge and wandered
across the field, his hair all
messy and his coat covered in
bits of fertilizer. He ate a stale loaf
from the bin behind the bakery
and washed his face in the
drinking fountain. He
swang on the
rope above
the stream.
He sat on
the bridge
above the
bypass
watching the
traffic zoom under
him.

Perhaps he could live forever like
this. No worries, no hassles, the
kid had said. He was looking after
all that now. But Porky was
cold and the loaf was hard
as wood. He wanted hot
chocolate and a fire.

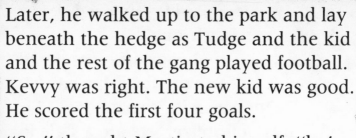

Later, he walked up to the park and lay beneath the hedge as Tudge and the kid and the rest of the gang played football. Kevvy was right. The new kid was good. He scored the first four goals.

"So," thought Martin to himself, "he's *not* like me; not *completely* like me. I've never scored four goals against Tudge and Kevvy." Except . . . Martin watched the new kid more closely and realized something.

It wasn't that he played better than the real Martin could. He wasn't any more skilful. He wasn't any stronger. He wasn't faster on his feet.

No. It was just that he was more confident. He really went for it, every time. He got stuck in. If someone took the ball off him, he chased them and got it back. If he got knocked down, he leapt to his feet straight away. He dived, he slid, he jumped, he ran hell for leather.

And Martin thought,
"That could have been
me. I could have scored
those goals. I could
have put a burger down
that snotty kid's trousers.
I could have joined the
swimming club.

I could
have made
Trish laugh."

But it was too
late now. He'd
missed his chance.

He slept in the shed again that night.
And the night after. And the
night after that. His clothes
were getting tatty and he
was beginning to
smell like old
socks.

No-one seemed to notice him when he wandered round town. Either that or they thought he was crazy and steered clear. He heard one old lady say, "Ooh dear, that boy pongs a bit." But that was all.

He really was invisible now.

He gave up following the new Martin Philips. He already knew how much everyone liked him. There was no need to go rubbing his nose in it.

On Saturday afternoon, he was sitting in the shed looking at his hands. He thought he could almost see through them, as if they were becoming transparent like a ghost's hands. But that couldn't be true. People didn't *really* fade away, did they?

Perhaps he was seeing things. Perhaps the cold and the lack of food had sent his brain funny.

He flopped on to the fertilizer bags and wished as hard as he could that it was all over. He wished that the kid who had taken over his life would disappear in a puff of smoke. He wished that Mum and Dad would come down to the shed and find him. He wished he could have a huge, hot bath . . .

A puff of smoke! He suddenly remembered. Aladdin! The panto!

48

Tonight was the night! He had completely forgotten. Mum and Dad would be there. Trish would be dolled up as the Sultan's daughter. And that kid would be playing the genie in front of three hundred people.

Martin didn't know why, but this made him angrier than anything else. He felt cheated. The other kid was going to get all the applause, all the congratulations, all the stardom. Why not *him*? Why not the *real* Martin Philips?

All it took was confidence. He remembered watching the other kid playing football. All you had to do was to be confident, to get stuck in, to go for it.

Three weeks ago he had been scared to death about acting in the panto. It seemed really stupid now. If you could live in a shed at the bottom of the garden for a week, eating wormy apples and stealing bread, like a bandit or a runaway, then . . . well, standing up on stage with your wobbly bits on show was nothing.

Martin stood up. He was going to go for it. He was going to get stuck in like no-one had got stuck into anything before. That kid, that fake, that copy-cat was not going to appear on that stage pretending to be *him*. Martin, the real Martin, was going to take a bow in front of those footlights; and heaven help anyone who tried to
stop him.

He knocked the window out of its frame, wriggled through the hole, dropped on to the vegetable patch, plunged through the hedge and began sprinting over the field.

Chapter Five

Oomph

He started to panic.
Maybe he was
too late.
Maybe the
show had
already begun.

The shop flew past.
The petrol
station and
the cinema
flew past.
He felt weak
and woozy,
as if he was gliding through the air.

He skidded through the school gates. The car-park was full and he could hear the recorder group playing Aladdin's theme inside the hall. He ran to the nearest window and pressed his face to the glass.

The panto was in full swing. Aladdin had been taken away by the sorcerer. He had gone down into the underworld garden. He had come back with the magic oil-lamp and his pockets stuffed with jewels. The sorcerer had tricked him and locked him underground, but he had escaped. He was now back at home with his mother and they were poor and hungry again.

Tudge, in his Aladdin costume, walked to the front of the stage and picked up the lamp.

He was about to summon the genie!

Martin jumped away from the window and ran round the back of the hall. The fire-exit was open. He burst in and bounded up the stairs. He didn't care if anyone saw him, no-one did. They were too busy arranging their turbans and putting on make-up and carrying cardboard palm trees.

He slid to a halt at the side of the stage.

Out in front of the scenery, Tudge said,

Look, Mother. There is a genie in here who will solve all our problems.

Sarah Butts, who was doing the curtains, turned and saw Martin standing next to her. She looked at him goggle-eyed and said, "Porky you're meant to be . . . I mean . . . aren't you. . . ?"

There was a flash of light and the smoke canister went off. The stage was suddenly covered by clouds of thick, white fog. In the middle of the fog, Martin saw the other kid rise up out of the hole in the stage with his arms in the air.

He didn't
stop to think.
He raced out
into the smoke.
He swung his fist
and punched the
genie as hard as
he could.

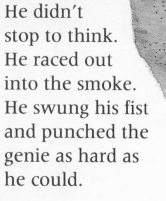

His hand went straight
through.

Martin tried to grab the other kid round
the waist and shove him back into the
hole. But there was nothing to get
hold of. The other kid was
disappearing. No, not
disappearing. The
other kid was
melting into
Martin. The
two Porky
Philips
were
turning
into
one
boy.

The smoke cleared and Martin found himself standing on his own in the middle of the stage. There was a long, stunned silence. Tudge muttered under his breath, "What the hell are you wearing, Porky?"

Martin looked down and saw his tattered coat, his grubby trousers, his shirt covered in fertilizer stains. Down in the front row, a little girl's voice said, "He's not a genie, Mummy!" and the rest of the audience began to chuckle.

It was odd. Martin didn't feel embarrassed, or small, or useless. There was something inside him which had never been there before, something confident, something gutsy, something like . . . like oomph.

He threw his coat away, tore off his shirt, and dropped his trousers. He strode to the front of the stage in his racing-car patterned boxer-shorts and pointed at the cheeky little girl.

You'd be dirty and scruffy, too, if you'd spent two hundred years squashed inside an oil~lamp!

he bellowed at her in his loudest genie-voice.

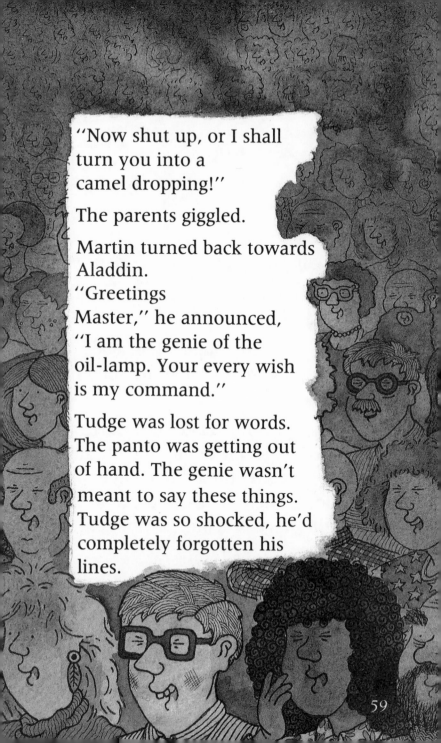

"Now shut up, or I shall turn you into a camel dropping!"

The parents giggled.

Martin turned back towards Aladdin.
"Greetings Master," he announced, "I am the genie of the oil-lamp. Your every wish is my command."

Tudge was lost for words. The panto was getting out of hand. The genie wasn't meant to say these things. Tudge was so shocked, he'd completely forgotten his lines.

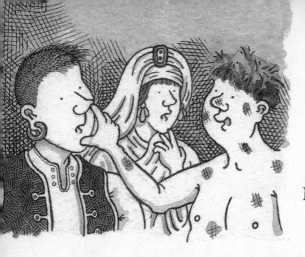

"Speak up!" shouted Martin. "I haven't got all day. Do you want me to take the wheels off the headmaster's car for you?"

Tudge went pale. The audience laughed and applauded.

"Er, no . . ." said Tudge, "I, er, well. Oh, yes! Bring my mother and me something to eat. We are poor and hungry."

"Coming right up!" said Martin. He walked offstage, picked up the big silver dishes heaped with food and gave them to Aladdin. Then he disappeared back under the stage in a puff of smoke.

The audience loved him.

Aladdin rubbed his lamp and asked for more food. The genie told him that he was a greedy pig.

Aladdin rubbed his lamp and asked the genie to fetch the Sultan's daughter, because he wanted to marry her. The genie said he was an idiot. The Sultan's daughter was a spoilt little madam that no sensible person would want to marry.

Aladdin rubbed his lamp and asked for a palace to be built overnight. The genie complained and said that it would be even harder than doing Miss Cardigan's homework.

With all the extra lines that Martin made up on the spot, and the laughter that followed them, the panto lasted a good deal longer than it should have done. At the end, when the actors came back on stage to take a bow, Martin got a standing ovation.

"You were brilliant!" said Mum hugging him. "A proper little Laurence Olivier!"

"I haven't had such a good evening in years," said Dad, clapping him on the back.

Martin glanced out of the corner of his eye and saw Trish storming towards him. She was waving one of the Sultan's guards' plastic swords above her head. She looked furious. He was going to get clobbered.

"How *could* you. . . !" she was shouting.

Miss Cardigan saved him. She stepped between them and gave Martin an extremely stern look.

"I ought to be very cross with you, Martin Philips," she tutted. "You completely changed the play – without asking me. You could have ruined it completely."

"Sorry," he said.

"But . . ." she began to smile. "But, you were the star, Martin. They loved you."

Trish dropped the plastic sword and humphed off towards the dressing room, and Martin grinned so hard he thought his face might crack into two pieces.

"Mum?" he asked.

"What, love?"

"I'd like a big, hot bath, an extra large mug of tea and a huge fry-up."

"I think that can be arranged," she smiled.

"If the famous actor would like to put some warm clothes over his boxer shorts," added Dad, "his chauffeur will drive him home."

Martin soaked in the bath for half an hour, sipping his tea, until he smelled the wafts of frying bacon coming up the stairs. He took the plug out, and climbed into his huge, fluffy dressing gown.

He walked over to the sink and stared into the mirror. "You're a brilliant genie," he said. For a split-second, he thought his reflection winked back at him. For a split-second, he thought the reflection said, ". . . and a pretty good Martin Philips." But he couldn't be sure. And he was too hungry to care.

He opened the door and followed the bacon smell downstairs.

Some other Puffin Chillers

CHILLERS

Clive and the Missing Finger

Sarah Garland

What has happened to Clive's strange neighbour,
the man with the missing finger? Why has he
mysteriously disappeared? And what is his guilty
secret?

CHILLERS

Jimmy Woods and the Big Bad Wolf

Mick Gowar
Illustrated by
Barry Wilkinson

Jimmy Woods is the worst sort of bully, the sort that likes hurting people. But there is one thing he's really scared of and he's about to get the fright of his life!

CHILLERS

The Day Matt Sold Great-grandma

Eleanor Allen
Illustrated by
Jane Cope

It was only an old photograph. Matt thought no one would even miss it. But he soon begins to wish he had left it in the attic when his great-grandma comes back from the dead to haunt him!

Coming soon in Puffin Chillers

CHILLERS
The Blob

Tessa Potter
Illustrated by
Peter Cottrill

The first blob appeared on Graham's book after
second break. It was a rusty red colour and it
looked suspiciously like blood.

Where did the sinister blobs come from? And did
they have something to do with the locked
classroom upstairs, or the strange new
headteacher?

CHILLERS

Spooked

Philip Wooderson
Illustrated by
Jane Cope

The note said 'Please help me', and with it was a
dusty old photograph of a pale-looking girl. Pete
tried to forget them. Then he saw the face at the
window of the empty house. The same girl's face.
Who was she? Pete had to find out, and that
meant going into the house. Alone.

CHILLERS

Madam Sizzers

Sarah Garland

There's something creepy about Madam Sizzers.
Perhaps it's just her sharp red fingernails and her
gleaming scissors. Rachel and Lola try to annoy
her, but then they stumble upon a dark secret. . .